This book belongs to:

For Jan,
with all my love xxx

Quarto is the authority on a wide range of topics.

Quarto educates, entertains and enriches the lives of our readers—enthusiasts and lovers of hands-on living. www.quartoknows.com

Author and Illustrator: Lucy Barnard
Designer: Victoria Kimonidou
Editor: Ellie Brough

This edition first published in 2020 by QED Publishing, an imprint of The Quarto Group. The Old Brewery, 6 Blundell Street, London N7 9BH, United Kingdom. T (0)20 7700 6700 F (0)20 7700 8066 www.QuartoKnows.com

A catalogue record for this book is available from the British Library.

ISBN 978 0 7112 5113 7

Manufactured in Guangdong, China PP122019

9 8 7 6 5 4 3 2 1

MIX
Paper from responsible sources
FSC® C016973
FSC
www.fsc.org

Hurry Home, Harriet

BY LUCY BARNARD

QED

Harriet was in a hurry to get home.
She was upset because today was her birthday
and it seemed no one had remembered!

"I'm going to make my own birthday tea,"
she said to herself grumpily. "I suppose if you want
something done then you have to do it yourself."

Harriet rode her bike to the shop to buy some nice things for her tea, including a very small cake for one.

She put everything in her bike basket
and set off for home in a hurry.

It wasn't long before she passed her friend Charlie.
He was struggling to put a very big box into his car.

"Let me help you," Harriet said.
Together they pushed the box into the boot.

"Thanks, Harriet!" he said with a cheery wave.
He drove away and didn't wish her a happy birthday.

Harriet felt even
grumpier now.

Harriet hadn't gone much further
when she passed her friend Flo.

"Can you help me, Harriet?"
called out Flo. "My bike has
a flat tyre. Could I borrow
your pump please?"

So Harriet propped her bike against a tree and went to help her friend. When they'd finished, Flo thanked her and then sped off without waiting.

"This is the worst birthday ever," thought Harriet miserably.

Harriet continued to hurry home. She was so sad she barely noticed the summer sun. As she reached the bridge she saw her friend Daisy carrying lots of bags.

Harriet slowed down to offer Daisy some help.
A scooter pulled up alongside them.

"Do you want a lift Daisy?" called out Arthur, from the scooter.

"Ooh, yes please," said Daisy and she climbed on.

Off they went, calling, "Bye Harriet," as they zoomed off.

Harriet sighed and climbed back onto her bike. Everyone seemed very busy today and no one had the time to chat, never mind wish her happy birthday.

She hurried home very sad indeed.

Harriet finally arrived home. She decided
she would have her tea in the garden so she
could enjoy the warm summer sunshine.

She opened the back door and...

"Oh my goodness!" said Harriet, seeing all her friends. "I thought you'd all forgotten."

"We'd never forget your birthday," said Charlie with a grin.

"You're the most kind and generous friend anyone could wish for," said Flo, giving her a hug.

"Happy Birthday, Harriet!"
sang out Daisy and Arthur.

"I suppose I won't be needing this," laughed Harriet, holding up her tiny cake for one.